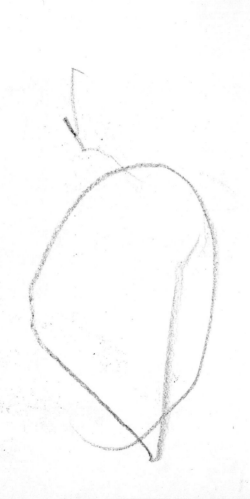

Mrs. Bretsky's Bakery

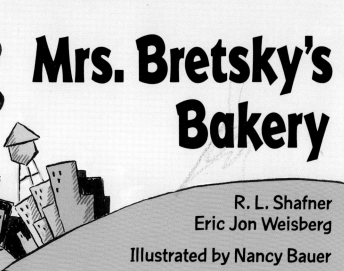

R. L. Shafner
Eric Jon Weisberg

Illustrated by Nancy Bauer

Welcome to
The State of
PUNSYLVANIA

Lerner Publications Company • Minneapolis

To our nieces and nephews — R.L.S. & E.J.W.
To Mr. Neil, King of the Peanut Butter Meal — N.B.

Copyright © 1993 by Lerner Publications Company

Library of Congress Cataloging-in-Publication Data

Shafner, R. L.
     Mrs. Bretsky's bakery / R. L. Shafner, Eric Jon Weisberg.
          p.   cm. — (The state of Punsylvania)
     Summary: Mrs. Bretsky, Punsylvania's hardworking baker who never
loafs, celebrates her birthday.
     ISBN 0-8225-2102-4 (lib. bdg.)
     (1. Bakers and bakeries—Fiction. 2. Birthdays—Fiction. 3. Puns and
punning—Fiction.) I. Weisberg, Eric Jon. II. Bauer, Nancy. III. Title.
IV. Series: Shafner, R. L. The state of Punsylvania.
PZ7.S52774Mr   1993
(Fic)—dc20   92-44338
                                                                   CIP
                                                                    AC

Manufactured in the United States of America

1 2 3 4 5 6 – P/SP – 98 97 96 95 94 93

Mrs. Bretsky owns a bakery. She's Punsylvania's leading breadwinner.

Why?

"Because," she says, "I make lots of dough."

Mrs. Bretsky bakes bread for everyone in the state. She makes a million loaves of bread a day, give or take a slice. Mrs. Bretsky admits she is a little flaky. "But," she says, "I NEVER loaf."

Mrs. Bretsky is friendly, too.
When she sees you, she will ask,
"What's cooking, sweets?"
Then she'll give you a hot
fresh roll, right out of
the oven. She'll say,
"Popover. Anytime."

Mrs. Bretsky has lots of friends. Why? "Because," she says, "I mix well with all kinds of people. And I don't get stirred up too easily."

"I don't cry over spilled milk," she adds.
"And I never put all my eggs in one basket."
Mrs. Bretsky is definitely funny.
"I have a rye sense
of humor," she
explains.

Early every morning, a thousand delivery trucks
arrive to pick up the bread at her bakery.
The truck drivers line up their trucks neatly,
one behind the other.

"Well done!" Mrs. Bretsky calls out as she hands the drivers their bread.

The truck drivers cannot believe that Mrs. Bretsky has baked so much. "How do you do it?" they ask when they pick up their bread. "You must feel beat." "I love my work," she smiles. "It's so full-filling."

Every day is a special day for Mrs. Bretsky.
But today is especially special.
Today is Mrs. Bretsky's birthday.

She should be happy, but something is eating at her. None of her friends have dropped by to say "Happy Birthday." The bakery has been deserted all day long.

Just as she decides to go home, her friend
Ginger drops by.
"Su-gar," Ginger says to Mrs. Bretsky,
"you look so cool in a bun!"

"Don't try to butter me up," Mrs. Bretsky says.
"I'm not!" Ginger snaps. "What's wrong?
Didn't the day pan out okay?"
"I'm fed up," Mrs. Bretsky sighs.
"No one dropped by for my birthday!"
Ginger measures her words carefully.
"Well, don't worry," she says,
"I'll spice up your day."

She whisks her
friend Mrs. Bretsky
over to her house.

When Ginger arrives at home, her door is ajar.
"Something," she whispers to Mrs. Bretsky,
"is not right here."
Ginger tries not
to smile.

Suddenly, the door opens wide! And Ginger
and the rest of Mrs. Bretsky's friends—
all the truck drivers and all her customers
and everyone else who loves her—
shout . . .

"SURPRISE! SURPRISE and HAPPY BIRTHDAY, MRS. BRETSKY!"

"These people," Mrs. Bretsky says to herself, "are the crème de la crème."

A birthday cake is carried in. It takes a lot of
people to carry it. At least a baker's dozen.
It looks like a pound cake.
But it must weigh
a ton.

Mrs. Bretsky is bowled over.

The cake is BIG. But that's okay, because
Mrs. Bretsky is
BIG too.

"HAPPY BIRTHDAY!" Mrs. Bretsky's friends
continue to shout.
"HURRAY FOR
MRS. BRETSKY!"

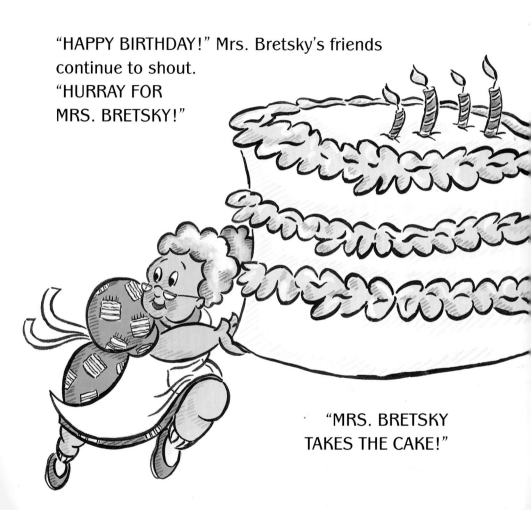

"MRS. BRETSKY
TAKES THE CAKE!"

Mrs. Bretsky is happy.
She knows that she's lucky to have
lots of friends who love her.

"Friends are my bread and butter,"
says Mrs. Bretsky. "Any way you slice it."

ABOUT THE AUTHORS

R.L. Shafner has won a number of writing fellowships, including an award from Stanford University. She has published a novella, and one of her stories appeared in *The Signet Classic Book of Contemporary American Short Stories.* She is now writing a novel.

Eric Jon Weisberg's major influences for "The State of Punsylvania" are Rocky and Bullwinkle and the Marx Brothers. A graduate of Harvard Law School, he is an attorney for Szold and Brandwen law firm in New York City. He was born and raised in Philadelphia, Punsylvania.

ABOUT THE ARTIST

Nancy Bauer sold her first painting to the Louvre at age 3. At age 10, she received a Ph.D. from the U of XYZ, where she lettered in spelling. When not making appearances on late-night talk shows, she can be found basking in luxury at her seaside villa, La Casa Jumbo (NOT). Nancy is actually a graduate of Minneapolis College of Art and Design, and she currently lives in Minneapolis. She spends most of her time reading, writing, drawing, and tending houseplants.